Alfie and Pepper
Go to the Village Fête

The Adventures of Alfie and Pepper

Alfie and Pepper Go to the Village Fête

By Siân Lewin

Illustrations by Alex Robins

In memory of my brother Julian
who loved a village fête

Alfie and Pepper were fast asleep in their beds when they heard the kitchen door open.

Alfie stretched and put his head under the blanket like always, whilst Pepper ran to the door. The only thing that would get Alfie out of his bed was the sound of his biscuits being dropped into his bowl.

"Right, Alfie and Pepper," said their master. "Today we are going to the village fête!"

"What's a fête?" barked Alfie.

"Well, a fête is when everyone in the village gets together and has lots of stalls, selling different things," barked Pepper. "There is also afternoon tea, with delicious cakes, games, dancing, races, tug of war and it is lots of fun."

"Oh, that sounds like something I would really like. Plus, I am sure there will be lots of treats there too!" barked Alfie, looking rather hopeful.

"Oh, Alfie, you only ever think of treats, don't you!" barked Pepper. "The idea of the fête is to raise lots of money for the village and a charity, but of course it's lots of fun with plenty to eat there."

Alfie, Pepper and Master walked up to the park in the village, where the fête was taking place. The park looked so colourful, with lots of bunting, balloons and flags everywhere. The village band was playing and the children were dancing around the maypole, shrieking with laughter and having so much fun.

The first stall they came to had a large jar sitting on the table, full of dog biscuits. Alfie and Pepper had never seen so many. The lady on the stall told Master that he had to guess how many biscuits were in there.

"Wow!" barked Pepper. "That would last a whole year!"

"Mmm," barked Alfie. "Maybe a month for me!"

So Master guessed the number of biscuits in the jar and both dogs were hopeful that they would win it.

They walked through the stalls and there were so many things to see. Master bought some brightly iced cupcakes, a jar of homemade jam and some books from the book stall.

One of the stalls had a lady making lots of different shapes out of balloons. She called to Master and asked if he would like some balloon dogs. Master smiled and said yes that would be fun. The lady set about making them.

Pepper's was a bright pink colour and Alfie's was a rather fun red one. Both dogs were so excited to see themselves as brightly coloured balloon dogs.

"I think they are really good," barked Pepper. "We will have to be careful not to bite them, otherwise they will go pop!"

They walked further along and a crowd were cheering two teams who were taking part in a tug of war.

"Gosh, they are strong," barked Alfie, "a bit like me, when I pull on the lead with Master. He always wins, of course!"

They then came to a large area that had been laid out for racing. Some children had just finished their race and were being given their prizes.

One of the children looked at Alfie and said to Master. "There is some terrier racing next, perhaps your dog could run?"

"I'd like to race!" barked Alfie, staring very hard at Master.

"Come on, Alfie, let's get you registered for the race," said Master.

Alfie was a little bit nervous when he saw all the other dogs. Pepper reassured him that he would be fine and it would be great fun, even if he didn't win.

Alfie lined up with the other terriers. They were to chase a fluffy ball being pulled very fast across the ground.

A man stood at the side of them with a large green flag in his hand. Then he shouted, "Ready, steady go!"

Off they ran, chasing the fluffy ball. Alfie ran as fast as he could. He could hear Master shouting, "Come on, Alfie!" and Pepper barking with excitement.

Alfie ran over the finishing line and was so excited because he had won the race. "Well done, Alfie," barked Pepper. "I am so proud of you. I don't think I could have run that fast."

Master was delighted too and gave Alfie a big hug.

Alfie was very pleased and even more delighted when he was given his prize, a bright blue bowl with a bag of dog treats.

"Well, I think we need a little break and have a nice cup of tea," said Master. Alfie and Pepper had their water and shared some biscuits in Alfie's new bowl. Master enjoyed his cup of tea and a large piece of very gooey chocolate cake.

Lots of children came and congratulated Alfie. He was a very happy dog.

Alfie, Pepper and Master went back through the fête and past the stall with the large jar of dog biscuits. A lady was picking the jar up and her little dog was looking very pleased.

"Oh, we didn't win the biscuits!" barked Alfie.

"Well, you did win the race," barked Pepper. "That dog is new to the village and was adopted from a rescue centre last week, so it will be a nice welcome gift for him."

"You know everything, Pepper," barked Alfie "That's nice that the dog has found a new home and won a large jar of dog biscuits."

They walked home with the new dog, whose name was Buddy.

"I hope you are in a happy home now, Buddy," barked Pepper. "Hopefully we will see you out on our walks."

"Thank you," barked Buddy, "it's a lovely home and my owners are so kind. I am sure I can let you have some of my biscuits when we meet again, I like to share things."

"Oh, that's kind of you," barked Alfie. "I won some treats too in the terrier racing, so we can share those too."

Later, Alfie and Pepper settled down in their beds. They had enjoyed their day and loved meeting Buddy.

They were both very tired, especially Alfie after his racing. Before you could say bouncy castles, both dogs were fast asleep.